W9-BFB-279

My 1st
Classic
Story

Johnny
Appleseed

a retelling by Eric Blair

illustrated by Amy Bailey Muehlenhardt

PICTURE WINDOW BOOKS
a capstone imprint

My First Classic Story is published by Picture Window Books
A Capstone Imprint
151 Good Counsel Drive, P.O. Box 669
Mankato, Minnesota 56002
www.capstonepub.com

Library of Congress Cataloging-in-Publication data
is available on the library of congress website.
ISBN: 978-1-4048-6581-5 (library binding)

Summary: A retelling of the classic tale of Johnny Appleseed.

Art Director: Kay Fraser
Graphic Designer: Emily Harris
Production Specialist: Michelle Biedscheid

For generations, storytelling was the main form of entertainment. Some of the greatest stories were tall tales, or exaggerated stories that may or may not have been about real people.

John Chapman (known as Johnny Appleseed) was born in 1774. He introduced apple trees to Ohio, Illinois, and Indiana. He was a kind and generous man and a great American pioneer.

When Johnny Appleseed was a young boy, he loved apples and apple trees.

His favorite place to play was his dad's
apple orchard.

Johnny loved the way apples looked.

He loved the way apples smelled.

Most of all, he loved the taste of a good apple.

Johnny spent a lot of time in the orchard.

He thought about ways to plant more
apple trees.

When he was old enough to leave home,
Johnny became an explorer.

Johnny was not a regular explorer.
He didn't carry a weapon.

Instead, Johnny carried a sack of apple seeds.

Johnny wanted other people to enjoy apples as much as he did.

He looked for good places to plant apple seeds.

When he found a good place, Johnny would clear and prepare the land.

Then he would plant the apple seeds in neat rows.

The apple trees would grow and grow.
Then Johnny would sell the apples or
give them away.

Johnny had many stories to tell.

He shared his stories with people he met on his travels.

Johnny roamed the West for fifty years.
He had many adventures.

Johnny always walked barefoot.

Once, a rattlesnake bit his foot.
But his feet were so tough that the fangs
didn't break the skin.

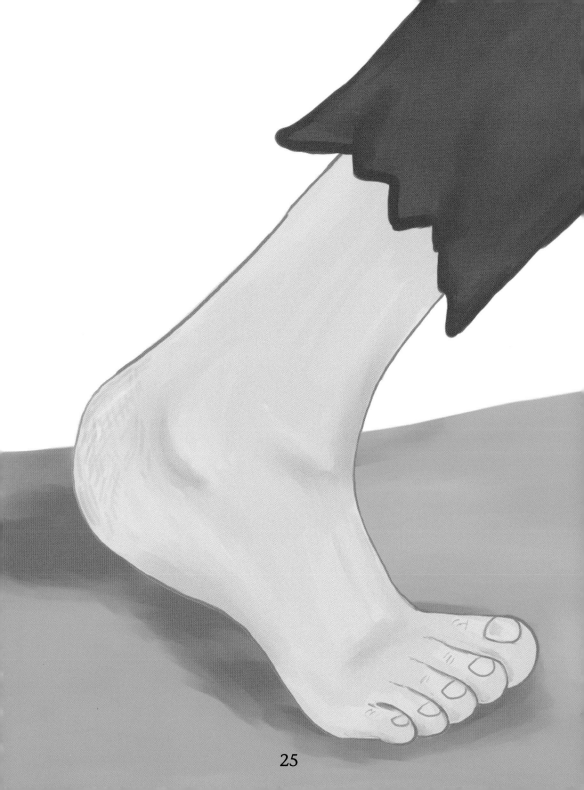

25

Johnny could talk to all the animals.
One day, he rescued a wolf from a trap.

After he talked to the wolf, it became his best friend.

Johnny also became friends with the Indians.

They enjoyed his stories and apples, too.

After years of planting trees, Johnny had many friends across the country.

The wilderness was no longer so wild, thanks to Johnny's apple seeds and his friendly smile.

The End